minedition

North American edition published 2014 by Michael Neugebauer Publishing Ltd. Hong Kong

Text and Illustrations copyright © 2011 Kazuaki Yamada
Original title: My Red Balloon
Rights arranged with "minedition" Rights and Licensing AG, Zurich, Switzerland.

Michael Neugebauer Publishing Ltd., Unit 23, 7F, Kowloon Bay Industrial Centre,
15 Wang Hoi Road, Kowloon Bay, Hong Kong. e-mail: info@minedition.com
This book was printed in January 2014 at L.Rex Printing Co Ltd 3/F., Blue Box Factory Building,
25 Hing Wo Street, Tin Wan, Aberdeen, Hong Kong, China
Typesetting in Optima by Hermann Zapf
Library of Congress Cataloging-in-Publication Data available upon request.

ISBN 978-988-8240-72-2

10 9 8 7 6 5 4 3 2 1

First impression
For more information please visit our website: www.minedition.com

My Red Balloon

Kazuaki Yamada

minedition

"Here comes the bus."

"Let's stop for Bear."

"Hello, Bear. Isn't my red balloon lovely? It's a present."

"Oh no, it's blowing away!"

"Quickly, follow that balloon!"

"There's Rabbit at her bus stop. She'll help."

"Hello, Rabbit. Have you seen a red balloon?"

"Oh look, there it is!" said Rabbit.

"There's Penguin. Maybe he can help."

"Penguin, did you see where the red balloon went?"

"It's flying up in the clouds," said Penguin.

"Oh, it's Elephant. I'm sure she will help."

"Elephant, did you see where the red balloon went?"

"It's way up there, just going over the hilltop," said Elephant.

"There's Giraffe! She will help."

"Giraffe, I'm sure with your long neck, you can see where the red balloon went."

"There it is, high above the mountains," said Giraffe.

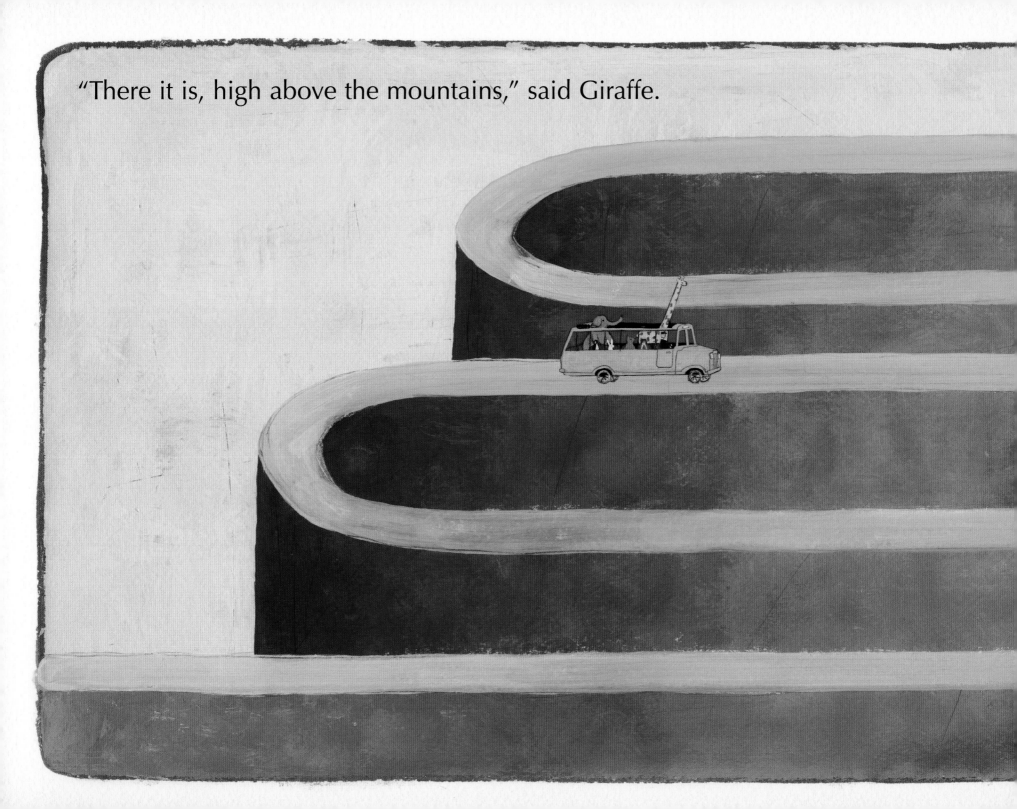

"Here it is! Hooray!"

"Oh no! It's gone!"

"Cheer up … "

"Look up in the sky!"

"It's another huge red balloon!"

"And we'll see it again tomorrow!"